Tales from the Canyons of the Damned

PRESENTED BY USA TODAY BESTSELLING AUTHOR
DANIEL ARTHUR SMITH

Tales from the Canyons of the Damned No. 26

All rights reserved Holt Smith ltd

Collection Copyright © 2018 by Daniel Arthur Smith

Catch and Release by Hunter C. Eden. Copyright © 2018 Hunter C. Eden. Used by permission of the author.

15 Things You Need to Know About Visiting the Spirit Realm by Philip Harris. Copyright © 2018 Philip Harris. Used by permission of the author.

A Peaceful Life I've Never Known by Jeff Bowles. Copyright © 2018 Jeff Bowles. Used by permission of the author.

Bus Stop by Ernie Howard. Copyright © 2018 Ernie Howard. Used by permission of the author.

Moroccan Fringe by Daniel Arthur Smith Copyright © 2018 Daniel Arthur Smith. Used by permission of the author.

First Edition

Special thanks to editor Jessica West

ISBN-13: 978-1946777683

Cover By Daniel Arthur Smith

Horror Fiction from Holt Smith ltd
Agroland
Tower

For Susan, Tristan, & Oliver, as all things are.

Catch and Release
Hunter C. Eden

WE'RE DEALING WITH A FAMILY in the suburban Midwest. Dad's about forty, climbing the corporate ladder and just starting to look longingly at the cute intern with the nice legs. Mom's a few years younger, but already wondering what it would have been like if she'd gone for that other guy in college, the one who played guitar and was planning on backpacking across Africa after he graduated. Brother's maybe eight, likes soccer, and is grounded for fighting at school, which at his age means rolling around in the dirt with some other little bastard he called a fag. Sister's six, plans on being a princess when she grows up, and practices hard for it now, the little overachiever. Now which one would you go for?

You probably said Dad or one of the kids. You figure that under your malevolent influence, Dad's going to grab a wood axe and start splitting heads, or maybe sister is going to start vomiting blood and talking about all the things your mother likes doing in Hell. I go for Mom. No one expects it because nobody pays much attention to her anyway. By the time they realize what's going on, I'm in too deep for them to stop me, and I can do what I came here to do.

First thing, when I swim into her soul on Hell's high tide, she starts to get really quiet. Sister's oblivious, Brother's a resentful little shit, and Dad's too busy thinking about that intern, so nobody notices. Dad tells himself she's just depressed, maybe needs a spa day or something. As my malevolent influence spreads, she starts eating raw meat. Next time they go to the pool, she dives in and stays under for two, three minutes, and when the lifeguard goes in after her, she bites him so hard, they have to close the pool for a day or two because of all the blood in the water. As he's getting stitches, he swears Mom had weird slits on her neck (and she did—they're my gills) but they're gone by the time she gets out of the pool.

Then the dreams start. She's standing on the coast of Hell, looking out at the dark breakers filled with the bobbing damned. Then my great, jagged fins break the surface like the sails of a cursed galley. Night after night, she sees it. She starts on the shore, then she's ankle deep, then knee-deep, then the tide comes in up to her waist and pretty soon, she's treading black water with the souls of the condemned, looking down at my vast, serpentine bulk twisting underneath her. Pride's not really my sin, but let's be candid: I'm glorious in my infernal horror. These soulless eyes like flat plates of crude oil; these teeth, long as daggers in a mouth grinning with sick whimsy; a set of hooked tentacles for a tongue...I'm everything you imagine swimming just below your feet when you can't see the bottom. I wish I could help Mom take a step back and see how rare it is to be possessed by something like me. She deserves to appreciate the exquisite horror that she's doing so much to bring into the world. I should just use her and discard her, but underneath it all, I'm a big softie.

We'll skip the consultations with doctors and shrinks that turn up nothing. We'll skip the moment where bratty little Brother sees Mom eating Sister's guinea pig with my mouth, chunks of its billowing flesh floating in her transparent stomach. That's when these dumb assholes realize it's not her thyroid or menopause.

What they need is an exorcist.

You may wonder why we do this. It's a lot of shit to go through just to spend a couple weeks inside a soccer mom, right? That's where the Mate comes in.

I meet *her* at a shitty motel with half the letters out in the sign: -OT-L. The parking lot looks like the high-tide line of human misery, awash with old McDonalds bags, used condoms, and needles. As long as we're being honest, I'm way out of *her* league. Wouldn't give *her* a second glance if we'd crossed paths in Hell, in our true forms. *She's* wearing a new number that doesn't exactly flatter her seal-like form: mid-twenties with his blond hair cut in a fauxhawk. A bit of a beer gut. You could believe he'd be curious about the harried but decently attractive WASPette I'm wearing. It's a bit more of a stretch to think that she'd go for him, but a decade of married sex as exciting as bilgewater and maybe she'd be desperate enough to give him a shot. Especially given how excitedly Dad talks about that smart new intern and her round, full qualifications.

"Hey baby—looking MILFy," *she* says through his mouth.

"Don't start that corny shit," I say to *her*.

"You don't want me to be your toned little pool boy?"

Some of us get really into this, like pretending to be some no-account mortal stoner and a bored housewife is exciting. If I wanted fun, I would've stayed in Hell. It never feels good anyway, wearing a human being. Less intimate.

She dangles the key from his pointer finger, the diamond-shaped fob swaying like a hanged man. Room 666. Dagon almighty, is *she* corny.

"Toned little pool boys do more sit-ups and eat fewer Doritos. Come on."

She sidles up next to me, smacks Mom's ass, and whispers, "I'm really loving this dismissive bitch act. You've got him harder than a priest in a boy scout troop."

"Look, we've probably only got an hour, maybe two max, before her husband finds her here. I get that this is your thing, but I'm here to perpetuate our unholy kind and swim home as soon as the tide goes out, so if we could hurry..."

His lips grin wide, the corners of his mouth touching his ears, showing off *her* needle-like fangs.

"Did I say boy scout troop? More like boy scout jamboree."

The room's what you'd expect. There's a big snarl of hair floating in the toilet and something stained the wall right above the TV a yellowish brown. As for the bed, well, I'm glad it's not my body lying there.

"Let's order some porn, baby," *she* says in her best dudebro voice.

"Let's get this shit over with."

By the time we've stripped down, I'm a little more into it. The big fishy eye *she* grew in his navel, unblinking and cold, the lamprey fangs on the end of his cock—you know how you meet someone sometimes, and they seem like a dud, but then you're surprised by how attracted you are to them? I'm not saying I wouldn't rather do this in Hell with someone else, but we're expected to breed once a century, so I might as well just relax and enjoy myself.

For all *her* corny bullshit, *she's* pretty good—even when we're wearing humans. *She* bites me, leaves big semicircles of needle toothmarks all over Mom's rough, skate-like skin. Bloody water drips from the walls, covering us as we coil around each other in the sheets, bedbugs skittering to escape the ferocity of our impure passion. I lengthen Mom's torso, lashing back and forth in ecstasy like an eel. I'm not making you uncomfortable, am I?

She lights a cigarette with his hands when we're done. If *she* wasn't as good as *she* was, I'd probably get up and leave, but I'll indulge this. I can't believe I'm doing it, but I turn to *her* and say, "So how would you feel about maybe meeting up in Hell sometime? I'm just off the coast of the Archipelago of Lamentation, and—"

And that's when Dad and the exorcist find us. It's too late, of course. Now it's time for the usual routine. A little holy water, a little potty-mouth, I swim home when the tides are right, and they think all that power-of-[insert deity here]-compels-you shit worked.

Except as soon as he comes in, I realize things are different. This ain't your regular priest, imam, swami, or rabbi. He's got a beat-up Bass Pro Shop hat on his head, and a shirt covers his big belly that says Women Want Me, Fish Fear Me. Half that statement is true: I'm fucking terrified.

"Here she is, Mr…?"

"Just call me Shep."

I know about Shep, and Shep knows what he's doing.

5

He has a thick chain in his hands. The hook is big and barbed, the size of a meat hook, and baited with a flopping something you might mistake for a small shark or a fetus, depending on how you looked at it. Those letters on the shank? They're verses in the secret alphabet of Hell and what they basically mean is that I have to bite.

"Can you do anything to help her, Mr. Shep?"

"Just Shep." He scratches his gray-streaked beard. "I think I probably can. Let's see what we're dealing with here."

The Mate draws back.

"Hey, man, I don't know what's going on here, but I just came here for—" *she* starts.

"Oh, yes you do." Shep sounds jovial. Just the way you'd expect from a man who took a day off to go fishing.

She strikes at him, emerging quickly from the stoner's mouth in a flurry of serrated teeth, but he pulls a pendant in the shape of a harpoon out of his shirt. Fuck.

"In Jonah's name!" says Shep, and as *she* recoils in agony, he smiles. "Looks like they're really jumping today. Now, you always want a good, solid chain leader. These bastards'll flat-out bite through a rope."

"Can you please just get it out of her?" says Dad.

"You gotta be patient, son." Shep gives a paternal smile. "Only way anyone gets good at this game. Now, we got a mating pair here, and they tend to get territorial, so we could probably hook them both if you want."

"Mating pair? Did he—did he get her…"

"Naw, they're like salmon, 'cept instead of swimming upstream to the waters they hatched in, they swim into our souls." He pauses, a reflective look on his face. "Which sort of *are* the waters they hatched in, if you think about it."

"I don't care about the other one. Just get Judith back." Dad shakes so violently, you'd think he was possessed himself.

"Well, son, we'll just see what we can do." Shep chuckles as he tosses the hook next to Mom's feet, and I can't help myself. The letters draw me out, and next thing I know, that fucking thing is buried in my jaw. I fight. I thrash around inside her, trying to dig the hook out. I could do it if Shep stopped pulling, but he won't, and the landwalking bastard's having a really good time too. "Hoooo-eeeee! We got a lunker on our hands!"

The Mate bolts out of the hotel room half out of the stoner, but Shep has the one of us he wants, and sooner than I'd like to admit, I'm out of Mom's mouth and lashing on the floor. I'm not giving up without causing some damage, so I lunge at Dad, who screams and stumbles back, filling the air with the ammonia scent of piss.

I coil back, ready to tear his entrails out.

The one thing that saves Dad from having his intestines unraveled all over the crusty carpet is Shep sticking that harpoon pendant in my face. The fucking thing *hurts*, a deep, leaden pain I feel in my eyes, my skin, deep down in my muscles. I writhe around, shattering one of the nightstand lamps with my bulk.

"I put this away, are you going to be good?" Shep dangles the pendant, sways it back and forth like he wants to hypnotize me. I don't have much of a choice, so I just say yes and tell him he can suck Dagon's claspers and swallow when he's done.

"Damn, boy, we got a fighter here! A real beauty." To add insult to injury, the motherfucker kisses me on the snout before he puts the pendant away. But he's right—I'm a symphony of despair and terror given flesh, and that's not such an asset here. See, all true exorcists have a trophy room, and I could be looking at hanging on Shep's wall for eternity.

We can kill each other, but you can't kill us. It's like being in a special club where you get to eat the other members. That was bred into us by Almighty Dagon as a failsafe so some shit-grade televangelist can't pull out a twelve gauge when the Bible verses fail. You do it to us, it heals in minutes, and we're fucking pissed off that you tried.

But there's a problem. Shep's necklace? They call that the Harpoon of Jonah, and it's the one thing you wormfood assholes have against us. You make one big enough, bless it just right, and you can pin one of us to your wall. There's no escaping unless one of you releases us, and the alternative is a harpoon stuck through you for all time. It's like Hell for demons.

I have to convince Shep to let me go, and my position is weak. You never beg, but what am I going to threaten him with? Way I see it, I've got two options.

Option one: buy his soul. Buying souls is a pain in the puckered and barnacle-encrusted orifice that answers for my ass. It's like a deposit that charges no interest, and then you have to go to the trouble of giving the seller whatever he or she wants: money, fame, the hottie they never got in high school, whatever. A lot goes on behind the scenes, believe me. A lot of string-pulling in the mortal world, dark whispers and obscene promises and sheer terror. Besides, what would Shep sell his soul for? What he wants is me on his wall. It'll have to be option two.

There aren't many exorcists in the world, and the number of *real* exorcists, the ones who figure out that a few spritzes of holy water won't do it, are a fraction of a fraction, and the ones who last without getting killed or going insane become legends to us—the sort of thing you warn your spawn about if you don't eat them first. Shep is a legend, which means I know a little bit about him.

Shep grew up in Mississippi, fishing with his Pop. He joined the army, deployed for Iraq One, and that's where he learned about all this. Found an old manuscript in a bombed-out museum and paid an interpreter to translate it because the pictures of hooks and harpoons, the map of a great and terrible ocean, the diagrams of fish bigger and fiercer and more dangerous than any he'd ever seen, it all interested him. Once he figured out what he was doing, he became one of the best—not because he wanted to purify the world or redeem himself or any of the normal reasons. He just loved performing exorcisms. The thrill of landing one of us got in his blood. He got attached to all this.

So in option two, I play on his biggest weakness: sentimentality.

"Well, Shep, it looks like you reeled me in."

Behind me, Mom is lying on the bed, gasping. I ignore her and Dad. This is all about me and Shep.

"Sure did. Haven't seen one like you in fifteen-odd years. Can't wait to get that grinning head of yours on my wall."

"Demons like me are getting rarer."

"You sure are. Tough to land."

Dad crosses over to where Mom lies on the bed. I snap at him, just to see him jump, and he leads Mom by the hand back to where Shep stands. She's swaying on her feet, only half here.

"Is this over? Do I pay you now?" Dad is still pale with horror.

"Oh, just whatever you can afford, son." Shep smiles and pats Dad on the shoulder. Dad digs into his pockets, pulls out a wallet with trembling hands and pulls out a handful of bills.

"Here."

"Well, thank you," says Shep, grinning. "Now go clean your britches."

Now it's just me and Shep, which is how I want it. He had to put on his exorcist face around Mom and Dad. Pull the Ahab and Moby act. But now I have him where I want him.

"You know, Shep, you're getting older."

"We all do. Well, all us mortals."

"You ever think about the next generation, Shep?"

"What, of you sumbitches? You're with us to the end of time."

"No, I mean you. You got kids, Shep?"

"You know I'm never going to answer that."

I grin at him.

"Yes, you do. And not just kids—*grand*kids. You ever think about getting them into this?"

"I wouldn't get anybody into this." He's pulling a net out of a bag at his feet. I have to do this fast.

"You know how long it took me to grow this big, Shep? You know what it took to get these fangs, these jagged fins, these soulless eyes?"

"That's why I want you on my wall."

"What about the exorcists to come?"

"What about them?" He's unspooling the net, and if he gets it over me—

"Don't you want to leave Hell stocked for them too? Don't you remember the thrill of the first of us you caught? The rush of adrenaline? Don't you want their eyes to light up like yours did the first time? Don't you want their hearts to do that happy, pattering dance of I-can't-believe-I-beached-that-thing?"

He pauses, and the net hangs in his hands. I set the proverbial hook.

"Shep, I'm pregnant." That's how it works. We both become fertile when we don mortal flesh, and we both leave with a belly full of squirming, embryonic horrors implanting in the sickening organ that passes for a womb. "I've probably got about ten eggs in me. One or two will hatch, and they'll eat the rest. Then it takes a good ten millennia to reach my size, and that's no guarantee. After we were cast out of the Pure Waters, the old fertility's not what it used to be. One of these little hellspawns growing inside me is going to get a younger Shep into the game. There's only one thing a good sportsman does here."

"What do you want?"

"For you to do the responsible thing. You're not in this for religion. What do you care? So you can hang me on your wall? That's not you. Catch and release, Shep."

He sighs, looks up from the net. He's torn. He would love to sit under me with a glass of whiskey, reminiscing about our battle. He maybe knows one or two exorcists, and he'd love to brag about me and show me off. But he's too sentimental. In a weird way, I respect him for that. It's all just for the sheer love.

"All right, but next time—"

I give that wide grin, rows upon rows of teeth, and he releases me from the Harpoon's influence. Then I'm swimming free through the black waters of damnation.

Shep will die any year now. He'll probably go to the Pure Waters, which is a disappointment because I would love to turn the tables. I guess he'll always be the one that got away. Such is eternity. Nothing to do but move on to the next soccer mom.

Hunter C. Eden

15 Things You Need to Know About Visiting the Spirit Realm

Philip Harris

WITH SALES OF THE iPhone XX reaching stratospheric heights, millions of people around the world now have access to the spirit realm using the brand new integrated RealmScope(tm) chipset. Now, convening with the dead isn't just for psychics and ghostwalkers. Anyone with an up-to-date iSpirit subscription can get down with Grandma Gerta or practice ukulele with Uncle Eustace. With the entire spirit realm open for exploration, you could be forgiven for feeling a little overwhelmed. Which is why we've teamed up with famed spirit realm blogger, Tanya Hurst-Jenkins, to get you up to speed with all things iSpirit. Here's the top 15 things you need to know about RealmScope(tm) and iSpirit.

1) Nathan G. Anderson, a California Institute of Technology graduate researching far spectrum light filters, created the RealmScope(tm) chipset in 2020. A miscalculation during the creation of a quantum lens resulted in a unique, and now patented, distortion in the sub-surface structure of a nano-wave detector. The resultant detector went on to form the heart and soul of the RealmScope(tm) technology.

The mistake proved fortunate, and profitable, for Anderson. The 1,328 patents associated with his research are estimated to have generated over $300 billion worth of revenue for Anderson alone. His sudden elevation to multi-billionaire status reportedly affected his mental well-being, and he has been out of the public eye for several years. Rumors persist that he lives a hermit-like existence on a private island in the Indian ocean.

2) Apple's addition of the RealmScope(tm) to the iPhone is rumored to have cost them $1.3 trillion. Profits from the iPhone XX alone are expected to exceed that within the next two months. Demand was driven, of course, by the now legendary appearance of Apple co-founder, Steve Jobs at the launch of the new device. His impassioned speech broadcast directly from the spirit realm to over seventy countries was not without its controversy, but the voices of the evangelical Christians criticizing the stunt and the RealmScope(tm) itself, were quickly drowned out by the exuberance of the Apple faithful. I was fortunate enough to attend the after-party for the launch, and the atmosphere was electric.

3) The heart of Apple's iSpirit system is the on-device DNA filter that can process a clean DNA sample and initialize the RealmScope(tm) in a fraction of a second.

Although there are already dozens of third-party DNA samplers, you'll want to stick with Apple's bluetooth enabled iDNA device available for $1,299. I've tried several different options and take it from me, none of the cheaper systems come close to the build quality and clarity of the results from the Apple device.

4) Whatever sampler you use, gather a range of familial DNA to calibrate the RealmScope(tm). I've found five good samples from living relatives to be the sweet spot. Less than that and transitions to the spirit realm become a little unreliable. Sampling a larger group dilutes the link and you run the risk of finding yourself bumping into inhabitants of the spirit realm that are outside your family tree. Save that for later visits and stick to familiar faces for your first adventures beyond the veil.

5) When you've finished scanning that initial batch of DNA, iSpirit will ask you to register your samples with a central database. This will prevent unauthorized use of your DNA to access the spirit realm. Ancestor theft and the rise of so called realm runners—people who take unauthorized DNA samples and use them to enter the spirit realm—make this an essential step.

It's true that privacy groups have expressed concern over the storage of so much personal DNA in one location and the potential for misuse by government agencies, but Apple has assured users that their DNA information is stored securely and access is only possible through your iPhone XX. Like most people, I was happy to sign up for an iSpirit subscription to ensure that my ancestors only receive visits from those I authorize.

6) A great deal has been made of spirit sickness and a quick Internet search will bring up dozens of supposed cures—everything from crushed dung beetle legs to expensive over-the-counter supplements of questionable veracity.

While it's true you may feel some disorientation during your first visit to the spirit realm, you will quickly acclimatise to it. There's no need to spend hundreds of dollars buying pills and potions (or hours digging around in dung heaps for beetles). Keep your initial trips to just a few minutes then gradually increase your time in the spirit realm until the sickness no longer occurs. A small percentage of people are unable to adjust, but if you're one of those unfortunate few then a simple travel sickness tablet may help. Just be sure to go with a non-drowsy brand so that you don't miss anything juicy while you're on the other side.

7) As you become more comfortable with the spirit realm and the novelty of being able to chat with Aunt Doris about her time as a sniper in World War II begins to fade, it's inevitable that you'll begin looking for other spirits to visit.

The use of DNA to visit the non-ancestral dead is currently a legal gray area. I strongly advise you not to gather DNA at random—there are already a number of pending lawsuits aimed at iSpirit users accused of misappropriating DNA. The most famous of these is that of Miguel Hernández, the Mexican immigrant accused of obtaining the DNA samples of a prominent politician and using it to "right the wrongs of the previous administration," as he put it. Public sympathy in Miguel's plight has grown, but there are other, lower profile cases. Don't be the next one.

8) Licensed DNA brokers are the answer. These accredited businesses undergo a comprehensive range of background checks and you can be sure that any DNA you buy has been obtained with permission, and that a portion of the fee charged will go directly to the family of the deceased. Contact the National Association of DNA Brokers for details of your local authorized DNA dealer.

And watch out for DNA phishing emails designed to entice you to provide a sample of your own DNA in return for access to funds trapped in an offshore account. These scammers are really just gathering DNA to sell on the black market. Fall for one of these schemes and you may find access to your family tree being sold to the highest bidder.

9) Celebrities are big business in the spirit realm, with the larger chains of DNA brokers snapping up the rights to such luminaries as Humphrey Bogart, Edgar Allan Poe, James Dean, and Audrey Hepburn. Visiting with those big names comes at a hefty price tag.

Marilyn Monroe tops out the list of most expensive stars to hang out with at an eye-watering $447,000 per person for a five minute group visit. Looking for some one-on-one time with the blonde bombshell? You're looking at an eight figure price tag.

Prices do drop considerably with lesser known and television stars coming in at the $10-15,000 mark. Still out of the range of your budget? A private meet and greet with Richard Sloane, who appeared as a background student in the 1988 hit, *Heathers*, can be yours for $199.

Oh, and if anyone comes to you with a great deal on a trip to see Elvis Presley? Walk away. The King's DNA has not yet been recovered after family members discovered the body in the Graceland Meditation Garden was in fact that of Johnny Lanchester, a little-known Elvis impersonator from the late 80s.

10) Do your tastes run a little darker than the King? Criminal DNA may be the answer. Despite considerable uproar from victims, the popularity of serial killers such as Ted Bundy, Aileen Wuornos, Jeffrey Dahmer, and even Tsutomu Miyazaki continues to grow. Prices are increasing but have yet to reach the levels of the big name stars.

Less extreme options are also available and shopping around will often get you a bargain. The International DNA Reserve Corporation are currently offering a 2-for-1 deal on Bonnie Parker and Clyde Barrow, and other companies often run similar promotions.

As part of my "Unlocking the Spirit World" series published in *Time* magazine last year, I spent some quality time with a *very* well known serial killer. Non-disclosure Agreements prevent me from going into too much detail, but the experience was both disturbing and exhilarating. If the idea of immersing yourself in the seedy underbelly of humanity's past appeals, then I highly recommend Darius Dark's DNA Emporium. Their customer service is exemplary, and they were even able to address a few minor concerns I had after my visit.

11) If you enjoy traveling, then a spirit vacation could be just the ticket. Tourists are flocking to destinations all around the world to sample the local cuisine and experience the spirit worlds of other cultures. The most popular destinations include Egypt, Japan, and Peru, but check out your local area, too. Who knows what spirits could be lurking right on your doorstep? Just be sure to

stick with a reputable company and ensure they are NADNAB accredited.

12) Although RealmScope(tm) is recommended for adults 21 years or older (19 in some states, check your local legislation), the iSpirit Jr. has proven to be a real hit with 9 to 15-year-olds. All around the country, parents are celebrating with birthday "spirit slams"—carefully controlled shows by the spirits of well known children's entertainers. Rumors persist that at least two of the bigger burger chains are planning to add spirit viewing rooms to their flagship restaurants, specifically to help serve this growing slice of the market.

13) It's impossible to talk about RealmScope(tm) and iSpirit without mentioning the rumors regarding "residual spirit feedback" that some users have reported experiencing. Since the launch of the iPhone XX, a few users have claimed that after visiting the spirit world they've found themselves encountering "disturbing sounds," "otherworldly presences," and "phantom souls." One user has even claimed they experienced poltergeist activity after using their brand new iPhone to talk to the spirit of a local murderer.

An Apple spokesperson confirmed that they have received and investigated a handful of these reports, but that the number of users seemingly affected is less than 0.1% and that so far, there has been no indication that use of the iSpirit and RealmScope(tm) device is responsible for anything other than a few frayed nerves.

My own experience mirrors their findings. Although I did feel some slight uneasiness after my trip to Darius Dark's, any disturbances I initially attributed to paranormal activity were nothing more than my overactive imagination feeding on the sensationalist news reports, and I have a second visit to the Emporium planned in the near future.

14) So, what's next for iSpirit and the RealmScope(tm) technology? Well, thanks to an exclusive visit to Apple's Haitian research lab, we can reveal that work on an improved sensor is already complete. It will ship as part of Apple's iPhone XXI which is expected to go on sale next month. The new system is said to improve responsiveness, battery life, and connection stability, but the big news is the new channeling feature. With the appropriate hardware, iSpirit users will be able to host spirits within their own bodies. Apple has not announced a price for the channeling hardware, but you can be sure it's going to be the must-have product when it's released this Thanksgiving.

15) Of course, Apple is not the only company getting into the afterlife business. Google, Samsung, and Amazon are rumored to be developing their own competing spirit realm technology.

Google's *Google Spirit* is particularly intriguing with anonymous sources claiming that Google's ad-supported DNA network will provide unlimited free access to the DNA of over 97% of people who have died in the last two hundred years—everyone from Charlie Chaplin to Adolf Hitler. Experts remain skeptical, but Google's stock has risen 27% over the past two weeks with the increase being attributed to the Google Spirit rumors.

Other, smaller, companies are also working on solutions, but they are not expected to hit the quality levels of the big four, and NADNAB has confirmed that currently only Apple's devices are certified safe.

So, now you know everything you need to make the most of your RealmScope(tm) and iSpirit subscription. Wherever your spirit journey takes you, we're sure you'll find it an exhilarating experience. Don't forget our regular *Spirit of the Week* feature offers a $50 prize for the best spirit realm stories. Just email us at our regular address.

Editor's Note
Sadly, this was Tanya Hurst-Jenkins' final article on the spirit realm. Ms. Hurst-Jenkins was found dead in her apartment last week. Police reports have hinted at "severe trauma" and rumors persist that her body was dismembered in a manner consistent with the crimes of notorious serial killer Tamara Samsonova. After much consideration, we decided to publish Tanya's final essay in the hope that it would serve as a fitting memorial to a life cut short.

Tanya Hurst-Jenkins was a journalist, blogger, and licensed spirit realm guide. She is most well known for her expose of the Seattle spirit smuggling gang known as The Dead Souls Society, *and for her books,* A Beginners Guide to the Spirit Realm *and* Beyond the Spirit Realm: A Dozen Lives Unlived. *She also worked as a consultant on the television show* Spirit Chasers, *and her work earned her numerous awards including* Best Newcomer *and* Best Documentary *at the 2024 "Ghostlies" for her work on* Beyond the Shadow of the Grave: Life after Death in the 21st Century. *She leaves behind a husband, Derek, and two children.*

A Peaceful Life
I've Never Known
Jeff Bowles

A PAIR OF CANDLES RESTED on the old leather trunk between Ronnie and Douglass. The room was dark, the air thick with the smell of pungent incense. Ronnie watched as the yellow flames flickered and danced in unison, bending toward Douglass as he took a drag off his cigarette, writhing and peeling away as he exhaled. They cast two shadows of him on the wall, bearded, overweight, fingers running through long, tangled hair. Ronnie found himself entranced by the image, listening vacantly to the dull sound of music and laughter coming from the living room of Douglass's private bungalow.

"I'm not a whole man. That's what they say about me. I'm really only half a man, or maybe even a quarter," Douglass said. "They say my soul will never rest 'til I'm worm food."

"Who says that, Mr. James?" asked Ronnie.

"They, man, them. The press, those worthless teeny-bopper magazines. Hell, my fans have been saying it since '66. But you know that. You're one of 'em."

Ronnie didn't know how to respond to this. He thought back to that night in 1966 when he and his family had gathered around the television to watch Douglass's debut. A shot of fingers flying over a fret board, a cut to The Darklings emblazoned on a kick drum. Then came Douglass's close up, and Ronnie had held his breath. Mad, murderous eyes, partially concealed behind thick sunglasses. Ruffled collar, leather jacket, cowboy boots and a sneer. Ronnie had never wanted to be a musician before that night, and he never wanted to be anything else after.

And here was the man himself. Douglass hadn't invited the rest of Ronnie's band to his party, hadn't singled out any of them with a nod and a proposition: I want to write a song with you.

"You know why I picked you?" Douglass asked.

Ronnie shook his head

"*Acta non verba*, man. You got some real fire. Got it like I used to have it. You played like a madman on that stage, like that two-bit dive couldn't contain you."

Ronnie smiled and shrugged. "Where's the rest of your band, Mr. James? Wouldn't you rather write something with them?"

"Call me Doug. 'Douglass' is for the newspapers, and 'Mr. James' is only for people who want my money. You don't want my money, do you Ronnie?"

"No, sir."

"And 'sir' is for the undertaker." He took a final drag off his cigarette then stabbed it out in the ashtray. "You remind me of me, man. I couldn't get enough of this shit either, not until reality set in. Fame is dark as night, man.

Pay some bills, Ronnie, have some fun with some people. You're only young once, right?"

Ronnie glanced at his guitar case. "I wouldn't even know where to begin," he lied.Douglass laughed a crackling, whisky-drenched laugh. "Good answer. Only answer a young man in your position should give. Well it's your lucky day, rock star, 'cause I know exactly where to begin."

The Indian was dead. I was sure of that much. But I wasn't scared, Ronnie. Nervous, curious maybe. But not scared. I guess I was about eight, maybe nine. I'd gotten out of the house 'cause mom and dad were fighting again. It was mid-August, southern Arizona, Fort Huachuca area. Hot as shit, you know? Bike riding on a dusty back road, I spotted a real nasty car wreck off in the ditch. Smoke and dust rose into the air, partially obscuring the old truck's twisted frame. Headlights gleamed in the haze, little dust devils spinning and pirouetting like Indian gals at a pow-wow.

I hopped off my bike, let it fall to the dirt. There was nobody else around, just me, the dead Indian and his pal. They sat against the truck, both of them bloodied up. Damn thing had flipped right over. This sort of shit happens all the time out on those desert roads. People get going too fast, hit a rough patch, and then *wham-o*!

His pal sensed my presence. His whole face was tore up, especially the eyes. They were bloody and swollen and closed tight. But he still knew I was there.

"How are you, son?" he called to me.

I didn't answer. Didn't think I should.

"Do you see my friend here?" he asked, smiling, his teeth all stained and caked with dust and blood. "He's not gone. His spirit remains. Come closer, son. He was never a man at peace. Always, there was war in his heart."

I can't tell you why, but without hesitation, I climbed down into the ditch. Could smell the gasoline dripping from the tailpipe. The old Indian told me to kneel in front of him, and I did that, too.

"Now, I want you to touch his chest," he said.

I reached out and felt his blood-soaked shirt, sticky pools in folds of fabric. My face so close to his, I kept thinking he'd open his eyes. Not like the whole thing had been a joke. Not like pulling my leg. I thought I could feel his spirit rattling away in there, slumbering and snoring, ready to wake up and make that old Indian dance.

"I'm going to sing a *hataal*, now," said his pal, "and I want you to sing it with me. It's his hataal. My friend never valued life. It is right that we sing it for him now."

He opened his mouth, and the most beautiful, mournful sound escaped him. I sang with him, following along as though I knew the song by heart. Pretty soon, I started feeling sick, like I was gonna throw up. My head hurt. It was like my mind had opened right up, like a breeze running through my screen door, filling my house and whipping up a storm right there in my living room. My hands quivered, my bones stung, my fingertips received a kind of electricity from his chest...Let me tell you something, Ronnie. That dead Indian? His spirit left his body and came into mine. He's still here. He's the one who makes me so crazy.

Ronnie stared at Douglass, spellbound by the intensity in his eyes. No words passed between them. Neither of them moved, and neither blinked. The only sound to fill the silence was the dull throb of music in Douglass's living room. Suddenly, the rock star's eyes widened. His face twisted and his mouth strained in a silent scream. He pointed at Ronnie.

"Boo," he said, then the rock star let out the most raucous, wild peel of laughter Ronnie had ever heard. He doubled over, laughing harder, nearly falling off the couch.

Ronnie watched in disbelief.

"Should've seen your face, man," Douglass gasped. "You get it, man? People believe all sorts of crazy shit about me." He wiped a tear from his cheek. "And the best part is, I let 'em. It's my favorite joke of all."

The rock star's laughing subsided, but Ronnie felt like a fool. He nodded at Douglass, fully realizing he hadn't been in on that joke.

"So come on, man," Douglass said. "Let's write a song now. Something with all that stuff they want to hear. Verse number one, Dougie and the dead Injun."

Ronnie nodded. He reached for his guitar case and undid the latches. Inside rested one of his most prized possessions, a firebrand 1934 Martin R-1 acoustic. He lifted it carefully and set the body on his leg.

Douglass whistled. "She's a beaut, Ron. Check out that flare."

Ronnie smiled politely and set his fingers to the fret board.

"All right, Mr. James," he said, "you tell me what to play, and I'll make it swing. How do you want it to sound?"

"Sound? Hey, man, I'm just the poet. I leave it to those other guys to do all the musical stuff. You tell me what it should sound like, man. I mean, you're the virtuoso."

The door burst open. Loud music, laughter, and harsh light filled the room. A young man and woman stumbled in. The guy was clean-shaven, his hair slicked back, a sloppy grin plastered on his face. The girl hung off his arm, her hand down his pants. She giggled and leered at him with bedroom eyes.

"I'm your girl, right Mickey?" she said.

"Sure, baby. Sure you're my—" The young man came to a dead stop.

Douglass slipped a cigarette into his mouth. "You forget something, Mick?"

"Oh, man. Yeah, man, yeah I did," Mickey said. "Sorry, boss. Using the, umm, using the…" He looked at the girl. "Why didn't you remind me he was using the, umm…"

"The office, Mick," said Douglass. He shook his head at Ronnie.

"Office," the girl intoned, "*offica, officae, officae, officam, offica.*"

Douglass laughed. "What are you guys on?"

"Oh, man," said Mickey. He bit his lip and let out a high-pitched squeal. "I mean, what a question. Like, seriously, what am I on?"

"Ronnie, meet Mickey," Douglass said. "He's my right hand. Watson to my Sherlock. Garfunkel to my Simon. He takes care of things for me, right Mick?"

Mickey nodded. "Watson to your Garfunkel…Watson to your…"

"You need something, Mick?"

"Oh, umm, the cops. The cops will come. They just will. And then … what do I do about it, boss?"

Douglass laughed. He raised his arm and flexed his bicep. "You shoot 'em all, muscleman! You shoot every last damn one of them."

Mickey let out another high squeal. "Cool, cool, cool. All right, I'll leave you guys to your, um, duties."

He pulled the girl closer and led her from the room.

"Duty," the girl said before the door closed. "*Officium, officii, officio—*"

The music and laughter cut out. Ronnie blinked a few times as his eyes readjusted.

"All right, rock star," said Douglass. "Come on, play me something."

Ronnie ran a hand through his hair. He closed his eyes and took a breath. *I'm not afraid.* No room for fear, not if he wanted to live the dream. His hand dropped to the neck of his guitar, his fingers finding their way to a G chord. He strummed slowly, softly. The G changed to E-minor, then back again to G. He played a few bars and opened his eyes to see Douglass grinning.

"That's it, man. That's it."

Then Douglass sang.

Electric, dead truck and red blood.
Pandemic, dead man, a new drug.

You see him sitting, a soul to share?
Two minds blown out by desert air?
He gave himself, his life, his kind.
He gave and took, one heart, two minds.

Ronnie let the song build, every strum and chord compelling him to play harder. He came to the bridge, the progression mounting upon itself then bursting into a sleek, driving chorus.

"No," said Douglass.

Ronnie pounded the strings. He let the song ride.

"Stop, man. Cut it."

Ronnie paid him no attention.

"Knock that shit off, you useless little fuck," said Douglass.

Ronnie stopped. The star's eyes burned, vicious, homicidal. Ronnie found himself locked into his gaze, a deer in the headlights, a lamb and a buzz saw, an insect about to be crushed.

"You stop when I tell you to stop," said Douglass. "I run the show, get it? I'm top dog."

Ronnie didn't answer. Those eyes of his, the power they held. *Jesus. Saying anything at all could be deadly.*

Douglass' eyes relaxed, his face returning to that calm, slackened, half-drunk expression.

"Sorry, man," he said. "I got problems, you know? Success comes with more problems than you can imagine. No choruses, that's all. I want it clean, just three sets of verses. And then maybe nine or ten other songs just like it, an A and a B side. Like a tone poem or a manifesto. You dig?"

Ronnie cleared his throat, his voice threatening to fail him unless he put some power behind it. "Sounds great, Mr...Doug. Sounds real groovy."

Doug nodded and closed his eyes. "Yeah, that's what I think, too. All right, Ronnie. What do you say? How 'bout some more fodder for the piggies?"

I murdered a man, just a couple days ago. Choked him out 'cause I wanted to see blue lips and bulging eyes. Did it in this very room, right where you're sitting now, then I cut off his pinky and put it in my shirt pocket. Sound good? Yeah, thought it might.

He came to our show at the Hollywood Bowl, just one of thousands, but boy did he make an impression. It was a real bad gig, man. We were really off our game. I drank too much, least that's what the papers said. Hell, we weren't even halfway through the third song when shit hit the fan.

Maybe I was slurring my lyrics, maybe I wasn't. But before I know it, these adoring fans of mine, they start hassling me. They cat-call me and boo and all that noise. So I stop singing, and I tell the boys to stop playing, and then when it gets all quiet-like and all those morons out in audience land don't know up from down, I pull the microphone up to my lips and shout, "You're all a bunch of slaves!"

They don't like that, not one bit. They boo even louder.

"Slaves," I say, "peasants, every last miserable one of you. And I am your new master! You won't need no English where you're going. You won't even need no German. I'm talking crucifixion, my friends. I'm talking whips and thorns and nasty-ass Roman centurions dogging you through the streets!"

It wasn't the alcohol, man. I was drunk, but not that drunk. You know who it was? That dead Indian. Most of the time I'm in control, but every so often, I hear them war drums pounding and I do all sorts of crazy shit.

Anyways, this pretty much shuts the show down. They start throwing crap at me, and then a bunch of them rush the stage. The cops come out from the wings and tug on me. Then the kids start tugging me the other way. It's like they all want to rip me to pieces. And then this one guy, this smarmy looking kid with great big telescope eyeglasses, stands right in front of me, sneers at me, and then puts a boot to my gut. I fall to the stage, and he starts kicking the hell out of me.

This goes on forever before the cops realize that, oh yeah, they're supposed to protect me. They wrestle him down and get me offstage, but not before I tell Mickey to get a good clean look at his face.

It was Mickey who paid his bail, and it was Mickey who drove him here to my bungalow. But it was me, yours truly, who choked that SOB and claimed his pinky as a trophy. You dig, Ronnie? So what if the whole thing never happened? You're intrigued. I can tell. They will be, too, those parasitic sycophants who buy my records but think they own me.

Ronnie hesitated before he played. He watched Douglass fixedly, entranced, suddenly having a hard time remembering what the chords had been. Douglass urged him on. He took a moment to clear his thoughts, then his fingers found their place on the fret board.

He hit the G, slipped to the E-minor, back again to the G. Douglass sang.

Pathetic, rock show, a black hole.
Parasitic, a no-show at the Bowl.

You see me kicked, the pigs just stare.
Kicked to the ground, too much to bear.
But still they work me to the bone.
A peaceful life, I've never known.

Ronnie stopped playing immediately. There was no way he'd allow himself to repeat that chorus. If he'd ever known panic like this, he couldn't remember. Even when he was a kid, and his mom had suffered horribly from her cancer, he'd never seen such malignancy. When Douglass finally spoke, it was like someone had sucked the venom from his veins.

"Yeah, man. I think I like that," he said. "A peaceful life I've never known. It feels right."

He opened his mouth to say more, but instead let it hang open. He focused on a blank spot on the wall, his eyelids seemingly too heavy to keep open. Out the window, down on the freeway, a police siren wailed. Ronnie listened intently, imagining a woman at Douglass's funeral, shrieking, wailing like the siren. Douglass's eyes opened. Ronnie was taken aback to see them full of tears.

"I didn't want it to be this way. I was a good kid. I've done some bad things."

"What do you mean?" Ronnie said.

The door burst open. Mickey didn't stumble through this time. He rushed in, like his legs had found their purpose. The music had stopped in the living room. No one was laughing anymore.

"It's the cops, boss," said Mickey. "They're on their way."

The siren grew louder still. It seemed to Ronnie that two or three more had joined it.

"All right, Mick," said Douglass. His voice remained subdued, his eyes sad.

"Cops?" said Ronnie. "What's going on, Mr. James?"

"Doug, Ronnie. 'Douglass' for the papers, 'Mr. James' for the parasites, 'sir' for the undertaker. And the cops, I guess. They'll call me sir, too."

Ronnie put the guitar down and got to his feet. "Mr. James…"

"Boss, they'll, umm, be here in a couple minutes," said Mickey.

"Sure they will, Mick. Plenty of time. I only have one more verse to write."

That old Indian was with me, Ronnie. He was there my first time onstage. I was fifteen years old, way out of my element. I wasn't scared, though. I was a poet back then, a real beat poet, just like Kerouac and Ginsberg and all those other cats. I showed up at the bar that night, and those hicks and desert rats didn't know what to make of me.

There was a band playing, a real buncha' good old boys. I told them I wanted to do some poetry between their sets.

"Poetry?" the drummer said.

"Yes, sir."

He glared at me. "You see these people, son? You think they're interested in the music we make? Hell no. All they're good for is drinking, fighting, and heckling hard-working boys like us."

He snorted and turned to walk away.

I was desperate, Ronnie. I had that fire in me. I really wanted it in those days. This guy was twice my age, twice my size, but before I knew it, my hand was on his shoulder.

"Have you ever been passionate, sir?" I asked.

He sneered. Man, I didn't know if he wanted to kick my ass or just kill me.

"I'm not talking about everyday passion, now. I'm talking about the everlasting kind. Love so rare it comes out of nowhere, a sandstorm, a prairie fire, an act of God Himself. I'm talking about love that only happens once in a lifetime, in two lifetimes, a dozen. A love so rare most people never see it, and if they do, they're numb for the rest of their lives, battered, broken, and spent. More than man and woman, man and creator, man and the universe and all within it. I'm a poet, sir. I'll be a poet 'tilthe day I die. That's my passion, sir. What's yours?"

You know who really said those things, don't you? It wasn't me. It couldn't have been. The sneer was frozen on that drummer's face, but I could tell he didn't believe in it anymore. That's what I do, Ronnie. That's what I live for. There is known and there is unknown. I'm somewhere in the middle.

"You got balls, kid," he said.

I got booed off the stage, but so what? I've been booed off so many stages, they all blur together. I'm a wild man, Ronnie. I'm out of control. And I'm sick to my fucking stomach about all of it.

Ronnie wasn't listening. Douglass sang without him.

Intrinsic, I'm drowning now, my final trip.
Deliberate, won't you join me for a dip?

A desert rat, one heart two souls.
A poet rat, fifteen years old.
Booed off that stage, worked to the bone.
A peaceful life, I've never known.

"And that's it," said Douglass. "Now we just need to sing the whole thing."

Police lights shone through the window. The two candles had burned down completely and were now little more than stiff white pools of wax stuck to the trunk's dark surface.

"What do we do, boss?" said Mickey.

34

"You know exactly what to do, Mick. Just like we talked about."

Mickey paused. He frowned, raised his shirt, and pulled a large handgun from the waistband of his jeans.

Douglass chuckled. "Mick, Mick, love the enthusiasm, babe. Please don't kill my guests."

Mickey hummed a few bars of some unknown tune then bolted from the office. He screeched at the top of his lungs, something about bullets and cocaine. A single gunshot rang out, followed by screams.

"Not my guests, Mick," Douglass casually called after him, "just the pigs, all right, man?"

Mickey screeched again in response.

Douglass simply shook his head and snorted.

"Mr. James…" Ronnie felt warm all over. "Mr. James…" It was all he could think to say.

"Shut the door, rock star."

Ronnie did so without a thought.

"Have a seat."

He did this, too, with shaking hands.

Douglass pulled out another cigarette. He didn't light it, just held it between two fingers. "It's a Roman thing, you know? Throw a party, invite all your friends, let them watch you off yourself."

"Did you really kill someone?"

Douglass leaned forward. He took a deep breath and scratched his beard. "Well that's a tricky question, Ronnie. To tell you the truth, I'm not sure who did what. A guy lives a life like mine, he deserves a little rest, don't you think? Is it really too much to ask?"

A deep pounding came from the living room. Douglass' guests screamed, but Mickey shrieked for them to stop. Ronnie kept his eyes on the door, waiting for gunfire, more screams, the massacre to come.

"Sing my song with me, Ronnie," said Douglass.

"Now? Mr. James, I don't—"

"It's not a request, rock star."

"Come on, Mr. James. None of this has to happen."

Douglass stood. He crossed to Ronnie, towered over him; he grinned, his eyes bestial and everything malevolent Ronnie had seen before.

"Know what else that old Indian told me?" he said. "A man's hataal forms an eternal bond. Eternal. As in, even after you're fertilizer. 'Cept it ain't eternal, is it? There's always a way out. You always got one more song to sing."

Ronnie lifted his guitar and smashed it into Douglass' side. He leapt to his feet, took two steps toward the door.

Douglass was on top of him. He sunk a fist into his ribs then, with more strength than Ronnie thought him capable of, threw him against a wall. Douglass stood over him, his hand clenched around Ronnie's wrist. He squeezed it 'til Ronnie thought it would break. He bent closer.

"Put your hand on my chest," he said.

"No."

Douglass squeezed until it broke. *Crack!*

Ronnie howled. The star pulled his limp hand to his chest.

"You're gonna' take this Indian off my hands, now, then I'm checking out. You just see if those pigs haul a corpse to jail. C'mon, man, sing with me."

Douglass began the song, and in spite of himself, Ronnie sang with him.

Electric, dead truck and red blood.
Pandemic, dead man, a new drug.

He felt strange, like he might throw up. His head was ready to explode.

He gave himself, his life, his kind.
He gave and took, one heart, two minds.

The pain built, raging, until he was sure it was endless.

You see me kicked, the pigs just stare.
Kicked to the ground, too much to bear.

The pain transformed into a vast, open kind of feeling. Ronnie felt an inflow of energy penetrate his being.

Douglass stopped singing. He chanted, "I'm not afraid, I'm not afraid, I'm not afraid."

Ronnie sang. He could do nothing else. It was electric, a force of nature. Douglass looked faint, his face drained of color. He bent low enough, everything fell from his shirt pocket. A pack of cigarettes, a book of matches, and something else. A white tube, as long as a cigarette but thicker.

Ronnie kept singing, coming now to the final verse.

Booed off that stage, worked to the bone.
A peaceful life I've never—

The LAPD broke down the front door. Swiftly, they swept from the living room into the office. They barked for Ronnie and Douglass to hit the floor. Ronnie stopped singing. Somehow, he could. He fell backwards, a deep knifing pain in his wrist. The police rushed them and placed him in handcuffs. More pain, but Ronnie didn't mind. The officers stood over him. They kept barking; they were doing something with Douglass.

Ronnie let his head roll to the side. He could see into the living room, more police guiding Douglass' party guests from the bungalow. None of them had been hurt, as far as he could tell. And in the far corner, sobbing, his hands wrapped around his knees, sat Mickey. His gun lay uselessly beside him.

Someone jerked Ronnie to his feet.

He stood eye to eye with Douglass.

"Didn't expect to still be here," the rock star said. "I guess that's showbiz, kid."

They led Douglass from the office.

Ronnie watched him go, through the living room, out the bungalow's front door, all the while, belting out a caterwauling rendition of *Thanks for the Memories*.

One of the cops pointed at Ronnie. "I want everyone checked out. You know what we're after, boys."

Ronnie suddenly felt so tired and frayed, like he was only half a man. He swayed, barely staying on his feet. He gave a solemn nod to the nearest officer.

"Can I sit, sir?" he asked.

The guy looked him over and nodded. Ronnie took a step, his foot touching something harder than carpet. He looked down, saw the white tube that had fallen from Douglass' shirt pocket. The police began picking the room clean, kicking over furniture, knocking on walls. Ronnie bent for the tube. *Paper.* Gingerly, handcuffed and with a broken wrist, he managed to unroll it.

A pinky fell out. Severed at the knuckle, perfectly straight, completely grey. Ronnie watched it roll then settle beside the broken shards of his guitar.

"Captain! I found something!" shouted one of the cops. He stood by the trunk, the one that had held the two candles, the lid unlatched and open, its contents visible to everyone in the room.

Ronnie swayed again when he saw what was inside.

Pinkies. At least half a dozen of them. Long ones and short, thick and thin; painted nails, rings, fresh-cut and rotting and some little more than bone. Ronnie heard something elusive, low and soft enough he thought it must have been in his head. He heard the sound of a wailing song, then the beating of a war drum.

He numbly raised the paper to his eyes, read the note scrawled on it:

For you, future rock star, whoever you may be.
For both of you and not one of me.

Best wishes,
Doug

Bus Stop

Ernie Howard

THE WIND BLOWS RIGHT THROUGH YOU late at night in the desert. It was especially bad when you had to sit on a cold metal bench at a bus stop with no barriers to block the damn breeze. I could always feel my bones chilled back then, on nights that I had no business being out. I'd go back to just being cold physically. You can do something about that. You can get warm again. I'll never feel warmth ever again.

I was looking for revenge that night. Revenge over something that most sensible people would have let roll off their backs. But just like I had no buffer from the cold wind, I also had no sense.

He'd called my girl the C word. Yes, that one. This was after she'd denied Scott Harmony's advances. The first offense got you beaten where I came from, and the second got you dead. In my neighborhood, you never disrespected someone's lady unless you wanted beef with her man.

Scott was bigger than me, so a fist fight would have left me beaten or maybe worse. He had friends who liked to jump in and one of his buddies wore those boots with the steel built into the toe. I couldn't fight them by their rules. So, I was off to purchase the inevitable object kids of my ilk eventually come into possession of. Yup, you guessed it. I was going to get a gun. And I was going to shoot that son of a bitch. I couldn't get one legally, being that I was only seventeen at the time, but my friend Brownlie knew a guy.

"Man, somebody needs to teach that punk Harmony a lesson. I told you what he did to my sister, didn't I?"

I'd heard the story many times from Brownlie himself, and extra colorful versions from people who had no emotional interest in the subject matter. I didn't want to hear it again, but I let him tell it before I asked him where I could get a firearm. "And that was when I knew he was a rapist."

That part always got me fired up. Why hadn't this wimp taken care of Scott Harmony a long time ago? If that had been my sister...Well, you know what I would have done back then. Luckily, I didn't have any sisters. I had Hanna.

When she'd come to me crying, I thought someone had died. She told me the story of how Scott had come on to her at Barry Larsen's party. He'd groped her in front of everyone, and when she'd slapped him, he called her that dreaded word. The rage in me came quick and didn't leave. Even looking back on this, and my past mistakes, it still lingers in the back of my mind. Hanna's description of the events played themselves out in my head over the next couple of days. By the third day, I'd decided to get the gun.

"Okay, so look," Brownlie said.

I hadn't been paying attention. I'd been watching the man-boy's dumb Adam's apple bob up and down. The motion of it was making me sick to my stomach.

"Winter? Are you even listening?"

I looked up, not understanding the question.

"Man, that dude is in for it." Brownlie laughed, and his Adam's apple bobbed up and down.

I wanted to punch him in the throat. He wrote the address of the place and I snatched it from his hand and walked to the door without even looking back to say thank you.

"Winter!" Brownlie called.

I turned and tried not to look annoyed.

His face was no longer amused. He looked very serious. "Get rid of the piece of paper. And the other piece after you use it. We didn't have this conversation. And when you see Mark Z..."

I looked at him, confused.

Brownlie motioned to the piece of paper I held. He'd written Mark Z and an address. "When you see Mark Z, don't tell him I sent you. Just tell him what you need."

I nodded and went into the night. Brownlie's door slammed behind me and the wind went through me. I drew my overcoat around my body, but it was no use.

Mark Z's house was on the other side of town in an upscale neighborhood. A neighborhood that didn't care much for people like me. It struck me as weird that a rich dude would be selling guns out of his house in such a neighborhood, but I didn't care about logistics at the moment. When I say the other side of town, I mean that the place this guy lived in might as well have been on Mars.

The gate that kept people like me out was tall. I looked at the damn thing and realized there would be no hopping the fence. As if on cue, a car came up and I saw the driver press his hand against the opener on his sunshade. The man gave me one snarled glance and drove through the gate. I followed and tried to keep to the shadows. I almost turned around and ran back to the bus stop when I saw another car pull out onto the road in front of me. But as quickly as I had the thought, another popped into my head—one of Hanna getting groped by Scott Harmony.

I looked away as the car passed me and kept walking down the street.

Mark Z's house sat at the end of a cul-da-sac. I say cul-da-sac, but the size of the houses made it more of a large, curved drive. There was no fence or gate around the house, which I was thankful for. I didn't waste any time but walked straight up to the front door and rang the bell.

Across the street, I spotted a guy with a black hoodie. I could only make out the bottom of his chin and one blood red bottom lip. The rest of his face was obscured by hoodie and shadows. The figure faced me and even though I couldn't see his eyes, I knew he was staring at me. I was about to ask the guy if he had a problem when I heard Mark Z's front door open behind me. I turned around so fast, my eyes took a second to adjust.

The kid standing in the doorway was blond and blue-eyed and about a year younger than me. If this was Mark Z, I could see why he was getting away with selling guns. No one would have suspected him. We stood staring at each other for a moment, my confused expression matching his. It only took me a second to sell out Brownlie.

"Brownlie sent me. Are you Mark Z?"

The kid in the doorway rolled his eyes.

"I told him not to send any more people. I barely have any more of my dad's guns to sell." The kid looked up at the ceiling. "What an asshole." He said through clinched teeth. Mark Z looked me up and down. He may have been young, but I knew the guy standing in the doorway giving me the once over was an alpha male.

He waved his hand, motioning me to come in. "We're going to have do this quick, my mom will be home in about ten minutes and even though most days she's out of it, I don't think she'd be too happy I was selling my dead father's guns."

"That's fine by me," I said.

Mark Z looked back at me with an amused smile. "My kind of customer."

All at once I realized where I was and what I was doing. My moment of clarity had come at the most inopportune time. I almost talked myself out of all of it, but my pride kept me rooted in the situation. It kept me rooted in my ego. I can see all this now. Now that I've had years to reflect. But as they say, Ignorance is bliss. And I was blissed out back then.

I followed Mark Z into a side door all the way in the back of the house. The room looked like something I'd seen in a movie once. It screamed 'wealth.' All leather chairs and bookshelves.

Mark Z walked over to a large metal safe that sat to the left of a gigantic oak desk. He quickly typed in a code on the keypad on the front of the safe door. The door clicked then swung open.

"I don't have many handguns left, but the ones I do are still quality items."

"Give me the cheapest one," I said.

Mark Z looked at me, amused once again. He reached into the safe and pulled out a small black gun. "This twenty-two is about the cheapest I got. I'll sell it to you for forty bucks with a box of ammo."

I reached into my pocket and pulled out my wad of ones and fives. I handed the wad to Mark Z and he handed me the gun. It had weight to it that I wasn't expecting. I pointed at the ceiling like I'd seen people do in the movies.

"Good, you know some gun etiquette. That thing is loaded."

Mark Z showed me how to put the safety on and gave me the other box of ammo that I threw away at the bus stop. I was only going to need one or two bullets and the six-shooter was full.

I was sitting at the bus stop feeling the weight of the gun in my pocket and the coldness of the wind when the man wearing the hoody walked up and sat beside me. I didn't say anything. The air felt like it got colder as soon as the man sat down. I watched his chin and lower lip from the corner of my eye. He sat so still that anyone walking by would have thought he was a statue. When he finally spoke, I went as still as him.

"Death is a strange thing," he said. His voice sounded wispy, like he suffered from asthma. "When you're alive, you don't understand how long it lasts. Death, that is. Not life." He took in a raspy breath and moved his arm up to his chin. Seeing the man move to scratch his chin looked odd and out of place somehow. Like it shouldn't be happening. "You want to kill that boy."

Ice ran down my spine. My heart beat so fast in my chest, I thought for a second it was going to pop out the front of me. "Wha—"

"You have a gun in your pocket. You're going to kill Scott Harmony."

"Who are you?" I immediately regretted asking. I didn't want to know who this man was. Deep down inside, I knew who he was. Or I should say what *it* was. I was sitting next to every ghost there ever was. Death had sat down to pay me a visit at a cold bus stop in the middle of the desert.

Its arm grabbed mine with lightning speed. "Let me show you who I am."

I was walking down a street I knew well. It was a street I was trying to get to that night. It was the street Scott Harmony lived on. I looked down at my hands and they weren't there. My mind was here in this moment, but my body had stayed back at the bus stop. I floated right up to Scott Harmony's door then right through. The sensation was nonexistent. I felt nothing because I wasn't there. I was only observing from the bus stop.

I was elevated to a position at the corner of Scott's room. I could see the whole of the small square of the dickhead's space. I watched the rise and fall of the lump underneath the bedsheets and wondered if he could feel my presence. I was starting to get bored when Scott's room door opened, and I walked in. It was me. Fresh from my travels. If my subconscious mind had a heartbeat, I'd have died right then.

I looked scared and hesitant. I watched as I walked to the edge of the bed and pulled the gun I'd bought from Mark Z out of my pocket. Me, the physical me,pointed the gun at the lump in the middle of the bed. My hand was shaking and wavered up and down. I breathed in and out in short breaths and stepped back and forth. Then the flash erupted from the end of the gun. One flash, two, all the way to the end of the six shots that had come with the gun. The comforter that contained the lump was still and the slightest of red was starting to form in the middle of it. The me who shot that sleeping lump ran out of the room. The me floating in the corner of the room stayed suspended and staring at the lump in the middle of the bed.

I hovered in that corner for what felt like hours. Surely, I was supposed to see something. When Scott Harmony walked through the door of his room, I started to come undone.

Who was under those covers?

Scott had a look of horror on his face. Slowly, he went to the edge of the bed and pulled the covers back, revealing a face I somehow knew was there. Hanna's dead eyes stared at my position on the ceiling like she knew I was there.

The pull back and out of the room would have made me puke if I'd been back in my body. Scott's house and neighborhood flew by in a blur to the point where I couldn't make out any landmarks. As quickly as I'd left, I was back at the bus stop. My body shivered but this time, it wasn't from the wind. I woke up slowly. My eyes adjusted, focusing on the sidewalk in front of me. I remembered the being who had sat next to me and I flinched and looked to my left, almost falling off the cold metal bench.

There wasn't anyone there.

To this day, I don't know what you would call the person...the thing, that had shown me the stupidity of my ways. I thought it was Death, but now I'm not sure. Would Death have intervened?

Whatever it was—ghost, time traveler, alien—it stopped me from making one of the biggest mistakes of my life.

As I sit and write this, my wife and newborn daughter sleep next to me. And I know now all life is precious and it's not my job to take it away from someone else. Even if they have done me wrong. Take heed, faithful reader.

Moroccan Fringe
Daniel Arthur Smith

JESS BENT HER WRIST FORWARD until the screen at the end of the selfie stick framed her, Jane, and Janice perfectly against the old rooftops of Tangier and the peach sky above.

"Okay," she said. "Say, 'Whiskey.'"

"Whiskey," they chimed.

She tapped the button on the handle, then retrieved the camera to show her friends. "Perfect," she said, then she aimed it toward Ms. Pimm entering the roof garden with the tea service.

Charming in her British way, the elderly inn keeper set the silver tray onto the sofa table, lifted the kettle high, then gently tilted it to pour the green tea elixir into the four spearmint filled glasses. "Enjoying the evening, ladies?" she asked.

"Yes," the three answered as they joined her.

"Do you record everything with that?" Ms. Pimm asked politely.

Jess lowered the camera. "Yes. Sorry. I should have asked."

"That's quite all right."

"She's a journalist," said Jane.

"A journalist? My," said Ms. Pimm. "Should I have a story to tell?"

"Not so much a journalist," said Jess, "but a blogger."

"A travel blog?"

"Not exactly. I look for the fringe, mostly."

"I see."

"Or a tea service," said Jess.

"Or the cityscape," said Ms. Pimm.

"It's right out of a Matisse."

"Indeed," said Ms. Pimm. "You know your history. The skies of Delacroix and Matisse were what brought me here when I was your age. Of course, that was a different time. The International zone was still vibrant and alive, and this house—oh ladies, this house was *filled* with music and dance, most every night."

"I guess we came too late," said Jane.

"Nonsense. Mr. Pimm, rest his soul, said *we* came too late, and that was the sixties. Before the Rolling Stones ever arrived. Tangier is a living city, ever changing. It's never *too late*."

"I believe you," said Jess. "I'll bet that the city is as full of adventure now as it was for Bowles or Burroughs. Just different adventures. And all I have to do is find them."

"Is that what you're looking for? Fringe adventures. I'm not sure I know what that may entail."

"I just want to see something different."

"Then you have to meet Bahi," said Janice.

"Who is Bahi?"

Jane laughed then said, "He's the cute boy she hired to take her to all the hidden places in the medina."

"He took me to an underground club you'd never find," said Janice. Then added in a whisper, *"The kif was incredible."*

"Kif?" asked Jess.

Ms. Pimm smiled. "She means hashish, dear."

Jane feigned surprise. "Ms. Pimm?"

"Don't be silly," said Ms. Pimm. "That was something we also did in the sixties."

"I don't think that's for me," said Jess.

"Well," said Janice. "He knows more than just that. I'll give you his number. You can see for yourself."

Despite the lack of a breeze, the scent of the jasmine still seeped in from the courtyard, along with a dull grey of the afternoon—not quite bright enough to cast a shadow on the tiled walls and floor. Jess leaned against a huge stainless-steel sink, the only thing in the ancient Moroccan room besides a black hose coiled to one the side, a small table on the other, and the bare unlit bulb hanging above. She was drawn to the indigo and ivory mosaics—she attributed the fascination to the light high she had gotten from the *kif* she'd sampled earlier. *How much earlier?* The room blurred. To keep her vision keen and clear, she focused tile to tile, her eyes tracing along designs that were a bit more dazzling than they should have been. By her estimate, she'd already waited twenty minutes when the outer gate whined open—but then again, she was a bit too hazed to accurately track time—*had she dozed.* The gate squealed back to a thud, then Bahi—her guide—ran past the open window and moved an empty chair from the doorway. He looked up at her and winked. When the girl at the hostel, Janice, recommended him, she mentioned he was cute, and he was. Jess smiled back, forgetting the scarf covering her mouth, but her eyes must have glistened, because Bahi smiled too. Then he waved to someone at the gate. There was a slow stammer of slapping feet, then the window filled again, this time with an old man in a white flannel pill box cap—the same kufi design she'd seen on the heads of all the old men in Tangier—and beside him, the perpetrator of the loud smacking footfalls, a shaggy golden camel.

As the old man ushered the animal through the doorway, a foul stench flooded the room. Jess had never before encountered such a smell. She fought back a gag and pressed her hand against her cloth covered mouth.

Bahi pushed in a cart, laden with a stack of folded sheets. He parked the cart against the wall, then went back out to the courtyard and wheeled in another, then went to join the old man. As he circled the beast—his eyes darted to her. He said something to the old man in Darija—the local Moroccan Arabic of which she understood so little. The old man nodded, and Bahi stepped quickly to Jess.

"He says you can watch," he said in a soft voice, then added, "It's best if you stay back, though." Before she could answer, Bahi pulled his thin cotton tee over his head, wadded it into a ball, then tossed it onto the top of his backpack. He was as fit as he was cute, thin, but not sinewy—athletic. Her eyes lingered over his tight six-pack and, when he pivoted away from her, the caramel tone of his delts. In another life—perhaps back in New York— he could have been a model.

Jess caught herself. He'd said it was okay to watch, but he didn't mean leer. He meant that she could record. That's why she'd asked him to bring her to what she called 'the fringe.' Tangier had been overrun by backpackers in search of a Morocco of Burroughs and Bowles that no longer existed. Jess was in search of what was hidden.

She snatched up her own pack from the floor beside his and removed a padded book-sized case and unzipped the zipper that ran along one side. From within, she pulled out another book sized object, this one wrapped in a piece of pink silk. She carefully folded back the silk to reveal the glass of her iPad, then pressed the home button. The white Apple logo lit the center of the screen, warming the room with modernity. She slipped the silk back into the case and the case into her pack, and when the numeric keyboard appeared, she typed in her passcode, then switched on the camera.

With both hands, she aimed the camera toward the camel and hit record.

The camel was glassy eyed. Its tongue fished around the edge of its mouth. Bahi cradled the creature's head, put his arm around its thick neck, and coaxed it to the floor. From his shoulder satchel, the old man drew a folded tube of fabric. He unrolled it on the small table, freeing a half dozen gleaming knives and small swords, then he unfolded the fabric—a full bib apron. He donned the apron and chose one of the blades from the table, a huge curved knife—part sword, part butcher cleaver, all Arabic. As Arabic as anything Jess could have imagined.

The old man approached the beast slowly, whispering a sing-song prayer. She couldn't understand the words, but his voice calmed her.

The camel appeared calm as well and spasmed only slightly when the steel pierced its gullet.

The old man dipped his forearms beneath the faucet to rinse away the dark pasty blood clots that clung to them. He softly sang another tune, more jovial than the first.

Bahi wrapped the last of the camel in a sheet then handed it to a boy waiting by the door. He whispered into the boy's ear, then patted him atop the head. The boy smiled, then bolted from the door to deliver his parcel, just as a dozen other boys had over the past couple hours.

Bahi pushed the carts out to the courtyard then crossed the room toward Jess. He smiled and gestured toward the coiled hose behind her.

"Excuse me," she said, then slipped to the side.

Hose in hand, Bahi turned on the spigot and pointed the nozzle to the floor so he could direct the pooled blood to the corner drain.

The old man said something to her. She shook her head to show him that she didn't understand. Bahi translated for him. "He says that you're smiling."

She placed her fingers to her lips. Her scarf had fallen away. "Oh," she said. "I'm sorry."

She pulled the cloth tight to readjust it.

"I told you," said Bahi, "it's okay. You don't have to cover your head. It's Tangier."

"I want to be respectful, though."

The old man spoke again.

"He says that you have a nice smile. You shouldn't hide it."

"Tell him that he's very kind, and that I like to separate myself from the story."

Bahi repeated what she had said. The old man ran the blade he used under the pouring water. He chuckled then spoke. Bahi continued to translate.

"Separate. Yes, he knows this. He says his grandmother was that way."

"What way?" she asked. Bahi repeated in Darija.

"He says his grandmother kept her smile in the top drawer of her…" Bahi paused and sucked his teeth in thought. "Vanity," he said. "She kept her smile in the top drawer of her vanity with her smalls, loose jewelry, and powder." He stopped as the old man added more, then said, "and he'd only see her wear it when she thought she was alone."

"When she was putting on her makeup?" asked Jess.

Bahi asked the old man. "Yes," he said. "The powder she wore smelt of roses."

"And all other times, she was behind a veil?"

Bahi repeated in Darija and the old man nodded, then gazed off.

"He's dreaming of a time long since passed," said Bahi.

Jess stopped recording and lowered her iPad. "My battery's about dead," she said.

"You need to eat?" asked Bahi, rinsing his hands with the hose.

"No. I mean, yes. But I meant that my iPad is almost dead. We've been here a long time."

"One moment. I'll take you somewhere. You'll like it. I promise."

"Okay," she said, then pulled the silk from her case to wrap and stow her device.

Bahi coiled the hose back onto its hook, then grabbed his shirt and pulled it over his head.

The narrow streets of the medina, crowded and bustling hours before, were eerily abandoned. The old town was shuttered for siesta, silent except for the purr of Bahi's powder blue Vespa.

Jess's tummy rose and fell with each little dip while a labyrinth of white stucco, cobblestone, and a tapestry of countless doors and window boxes painted bright yellow, red, and blue, of faded and chipped mosaic murals that ran house to house across the bottom of courtyard walls—all zoomed past at a dizzying pace.

Around one tight curve, the back of the scooter struck an out of place brick, abruptly bounced up, and jolted her stomach, prompting her to squeeze her thighs into the saddle and dig her fingers deep into Bahi's waist. She found his muscles firm and grounding—she wanted to let loose and apologize but convinced herself it was safer to no let go.

The ride seemed to be too long for the small area of the city, and Jess was relieved when Bahi slowed to the open-air café—one of the few serving in the afternoon. The Vespa skidded to a stop, then stalled. The sudden silence washed Jess with a wave of still catharsis, but the still clinging vibration of the bike weakened her knees as she stood.

"Are you okay?" asked Bahi.

"Yeah," she said distantly. "Fine." Her attention had already shifted to the interior of the café, specifically to the mural of a blue haired mermaid. Time had faded most of the mythical creature's features, but the cerulean eyes remained piercing.

Painted across the top of the mural was a blue-ribbon banner. She read the italicized words written across it aloud. *"La Sirène Bleue,"* she said.

"The Blue Mermaid," said Bahi. "It's the name of the café."

The café was really just two small tables and a coffee bar. Jess pulled her camera from her pocket and snapped a photo of the mural, and then chose the table beneath it.

A curtain behind the coffee bar flew to the side and a waiter emerged with two glasses and a pitcher of water.

Bahi rattled off an order in Darija and the waiter disappeared to the back, only to return a moment later with two small plates and a tagine—a shallow, mustard colored earthenware with a tall, conical lid which, when opened, revealed a plate of thinly sliced meat and potatoes.

"You're going to like this," said Bahi.

"What is it?"

"Taste it first."

Jess moved a small portion of the meat to her plate. The slices were coated in a thin orange sauce that she assumed was a mix of paprika and cumin. The meat was tender and she was easily able to break off a small portion with her fork.

"This is delicious," she said. "Is that cinnamon?"

"Yes. With paprika and smoked cumin."

Jess smiled. "It is really good." She put her fork on the tray to pull a larger portion with potatoes. "May I?"

"Go ahead. But tell me. Can you guess the meat?"

She took another bite. "It's too sweet to be lamb or goat. Is it, roast pork?"

"It's the camel."

Jess feigned surprise. "No. Really?"

"Yes. This is one of the first cuts. The boy brought it here while we were working."

"Well," she said. "It's really good."

Jess placed the cone of the tagine next to the meat dish then shot a picture.

The kitchen was filled with peach morning light and the aroma of the fresh muffins Ms. Pimm had baked before going to the market. Jane and Janice were out early too, leaving Jess alone to post to her *fringe* experience to her blog. The post was about Bahi, the old man, the camel, and how sweet and pork like it was as opposed to the lamb or beef taste she expected. There was no mention of *kif* because, she thought, that would be too basic—too expected. Satisfied with her story, she was set to publish, but she wanted to share the camel clip with Janice before editing and uploading so that she could see it first. It was Janice after all who suggested that she hire Bahi to show her around the medina.

So while she waited for the girls to return, she helped herself to a muffin and swiped across the photos she'd taken during her Moroccan adventure.

The bell above the front door jingled, signaling someone was entering the house.

"Jane? Janice?" Jess yelled. "Is that you?"

"Yes," replied Jane, her voice pitched and frantic. "Thank goodness you're here."

Jess unplugged her iPad. "What's wrong?" she asked as she headed toward the sitting room. There was Jane, along with two older Moroccan men in shabby tan suits. Jane's face and eyes were red—she'd been crying.

"Oh my god, Jane," said Jess. "Are you okay? What happened?"

Jane wrapped her arms around Jess and began to sob. "It's Janice."

"Janice? Where is she?"

"She's gone," said Jane.

Jess held Jane tight. "Gone?" she asked. "Are these the police?"

"Yes," said the man closest to her. "We are inspectors. We came back with miss Jane to help her find her friend. It appears she's been missing since yesterday."

Jane stepped back from Jess, wiped the back of her hand across her eyes and said, "She disappeared in the afternoon and didn't come in last night. They think Bahi had something to do with it."

"Jane says you've met Janice's friend Bahi?"

"Yes. I mean, he's more of a guide than a friend. She introduced me to him."

"Janice was last seen going through the medina with a young man. We believe this young man is the one you call Bahi."

"It couldn't be," said Jess.

"Why do you say that?"

"Bahi was with me," said Jess. "All day and into the evening. He took me to see a camel butchered and then we went to a café where they cooked some for us. If Janice disappeared in the afternoon, it would have had to have been someone else."

"I see. Do you have any evidence?"

"Evidence?"

"Something or someone that could corroborate your story."

"Yes," said Jess. "As a matter of fact, I do. I have a recording to prove it."

"A recording?"

"I made a video of them butchering the camel."

"Why do you record this?"

"She's a journalist," said Jane.

"Ah," said the inspector. "May I see it?"

"Sure. It's right here." Jess cued up the video and handed the iPad to the inspector.

The second policeman crowded to the first's side so that they both could see.

The inspector frowned.

"Just hit the white arrow," said Jess.

"Where is this?" he asked.

"It's in the medina. I'm not sure I could find my way back."

He then tapped the screen, and in an instant, his face went blank, the second policeman mumbled something horrid.

"I know it's gross," said Jess. "But it's just a camel."

The inspector's eyes creeped up to meet Jess. "Are you insane?"

"It's just a camel."

"It's no camel," he said, handing her the iPad so she and Jane could see for themselves.

Upon seeing the screen, Jane let loose a blood curdling scream.

Jess's knees went weak and her throat and chest clenched tight—breathing ceased.

All else, the policemen, the room, everything—swirled away.

What was on the video made no sense, it was impossible.

There was no camel.

It was a woman on the screen. A woman with glazed lifeless eyes and an open bleeding gash across her throat. A woman whose limbs were being methodically severed and wrapped in white cloth. A woman being butchered—Janice.

ABOUT THE AUTHORS

Hunter C. Eden is a Denver-based essayist and dark fantasy writer whose work has appeared in **Weird Tales, City Slab**, and **Ravenous Monster Horror Webzine**.

Philip Harris was born in England but now lives in Canada where he works for a large video game developer. Not content with creating imaginary worlds for a living, he spends his spare time indulging his love of writing. His published books include **The Girl in the City Trilogy** and an homage to the old pulp science fiction serials - **Glitch Mitchell** and the **Unseen Planet**.

His short fiction has appeared in numerous anthologies and magazines including **The Jurassic Chronicles, Bones, Uncommon Minds, The Anthology of European SF**, and **Peeping Tom**. He has also worked as security for Darth Vader.

For news and updates visit solitarymindset.com.

Jeff Bowles is a science fiction and horror writer from the mountains of Colorado. The best of his outrageous and imaginative short stories are collected in **Godling and Other Paint Stories, Fear and Loathing in Las Cruces**, and **Brave New Multiverse**. He has published work in magazines and anthologies like **PodCastle, Black Static, The Threepenny Review**, and **Dark Moon Digest**. Jeff earned his Master of Fine Arts degree in creative writing at Western State Colorado University. He currently lives in the high-altitude Pikes Peak region, where he dreams strange dreams and spends far too much time under the stars.

For news and updates visit Jeff's YouTube channel: Jeff Bowles Central.

Ernie Howard was born on January 29,1977 during a Minnesota blizzard. His two story telling parents almost didn't make it to the hospital in their beat up blue Cadillac. Ernie is the writer of *Write Something!,* a book about the illusion of Writers Block. *A World Without*, a Science Fiction book about the love between a husband and wife, and the darkness that can come into a marriage. *Walter*, A Science Fiction book about a boy who is an outcast who makes a friend with a man that speaks to him through his television. Ernie lives with his wife and 3 boys in Henderson, NV, where he dreams up new stories, and tries to live every day to the fullest.

Jessica West (a.k.a. West1Jess) is currently pursuing a state of self-induced psychosis, also known as writing. In the past, she has worked for Wal-Mart, a lawyer, and a bank. Now if she could just get a couple years experience with the IRS and the NSA, world domination is in the bag.

Jess lives in Acadiana with three daughters still young enough to think she's cool and a husband who knows better but likes her anyway.

For news and updates visit west1jess.com

Daniel Arthur Smith is a USA Today bestselling author. His titles include *Spectral Shift*, *Hugh Howey Lives*, *The Cathari Treasure*, *The Somali Deception*, and a few other novels and short stories. He also curates the phenomenal short fiction series *Tales from the Canyons of the Damned* and *Frontiers of Speculative Fiction*.

He was raised in Michigan and graduated from Western Michigan University where he studied philosophy, with focus on cognitive science, meta-physics, and comparative religion. He began his career as a bartender, barista, poetry house proprietor, teacher, and then became a technologist and futurist for the Fortune 100 across the Americas and Europe.

Daniel has traveled to over 300 cities in 22 countries, residing in Los Angeles, Kalamazoo, Prague, Crete, and now writes in Manhattan where he lives with his wife and young sons.

For news and updates visit danielarthursmith.com

www.ingramcontent.com/pod-product-compliance
Lightning Source LLC
Chambersburg PA
CBHW020317150626
46552CB00022B/2912